This book

belongs to

_____

_____

To George, Digby and Harry

First published in 1989 in Great Britain by Aurum Books for Children
Published in this edition in 2001 by

Gullane Children's Books

185 Fleet Street, London EC4A 2HS
www.gullanebooks.com

3 5 7 9 10 8 6 4 2

Text and illustrations © Peter Utton 1989

The right of Peter Utton to be identified
as the author and illustrator of this work has been asserted by him
in accordance with the Copyright, Designs, and Patents Act, 1988.

A CIP record for this title is available from the British Library.

ISBN 978-1-86233-312-3

Printed and bound in China

The Witch's Hand

by
Peter
Utton

GULLANE
CHILDREN'S BOOKS

"URGGH!" said George. "What's that?" and he
pointed to a horrible, brown, crinkly thing pinned to the wall.
Dad looked up. "Oh, that, why that's a . . ."
and he paused and looked down at his son,
"that's a . . . no, I can't tell you – it's too scary."
"Scary?" cried George. "Why is it scary? Tell me, tell me!"
"Oh, all right then," said Dad, "but it is scary."
And he lifted George on to his lap.

"Well," said Dad, "last night when you and your brother and Mummy and I were all in bed, I woke up suddenly. I sat up and stared into the darkness. I heard a sort of

slither-slither, pat-pat, cackle-cackle.

Someone, or something, was moving along the landing.
I slipped out of bed and crept to the door.
Listening, I heard again the

slithery-pattery-cackling

sound from down the hall.

I rushed on tiptoe to your bedroom. The door
was slightly open. I peeped in. My hair stood on end
and I gazed in horror as I saw a huge witch, dressed in
a great black cloak and tall pointed hat,
bending over your little beds.

By the dim glow of your nightlight I could see she was
horribly ugly. She peered down at you with an awful grin, and from
between her green, occasional teeth squeezed a grotesque cackle.
She lifted up a dirty sack and, as her bony hand reached out
towards you, I tried to shout, 'Stop! You horrible old hag!'
But all I said was,

'STORRUGORRIGUGGUGAG . . . '

The witch stopped, slowly turned and fixed me with a terrible bloodshot stare. Pointing a disgusting finger at me, she hissed a most evil hiss,

'Stand back, I must have these boys!'

'Oh, no you won't!' I whispered and, staggering
over to her, I gripped her large warty wrists.
'Urrk!' I thought.
Just touching her made me shiver.

We struggled for many long minutes in
a dreadful silence, until I was able to
grab her and give her a good shake.

'Uggle, oggle, aggle!'

she squawked and went limp and smelly.

'I've won!' I thought, but suddenly, with a blood-freezing cackle, the vile old woman began growing larger and stronger and more revolting by the second.

'Good gracious!' called Mummy, poking her head
round the bedroom door. 'Don't wake the boys!'
'Quick!' I gasped. 'Get the sword!'
'Sword? Which sword?' asked Mummy.
'Yes, the witch sword. It's in the broom cupboard!' I said.
'Oh, that sword,' cried Mummy, and rushed from the room.

'You silly little man!' croaked the witch and, bending her face
down to mine, she blew a sickening cloud of stench
and cobwebs into my face, and grabbed me!
'This is the end!' I thought, but then Mummy appeared in the
doorway, wielding the great sword from the broom cupboard.
'Too late!' hissed the witch and stabbed at me
with a dagger of vipers.

'Oh, no you don't!' cried Mummy,
and with one bound and a great swish of
the sword, she cut off the horrible hand and
it fell to the ground with its fearful weapon.

'What a rotten trick!' the witch screeched and,
with a squelchy-spluttery sound, she started to sink
down and down until, with a final, watery splop! she disappeared.

SPLOP!

'Phew!' I said. 'That was a near thing!'
And Mummy and I looked at you and
your brother still sleeping quietly in your beds.
'Look!' said Mummy, pointing at the floor.
There lay the horrible hag's hand,
all brown and withered and crinkly.
'I'll pin that on the wall,' I said, 'to remind
me to lock all the doors at night.'
'Good idea,' said Mummy. 'I'll make some tea.'

"And that's the story of the witch's hand,"
said Dad, and George gazed up at the horrible,
brown, crinkly thing.

"Is that really the witch's hand?" he whispered.

"No," replied Dad, and he reached up and picked it off the wall. "It's a leaf I found in the park the other day. It was a beautiful, reddish-gold colour but now it's gone all horrible and brown and crinkly," and he crushed it to dust in his hand and dropped it in the waste bin.

"It was just a story," he laughed.
George looked at the wall, and then he looked at the waste bin;
then he looked at his mummy and saw that she was smiling.
"Why, you rotten fibber!" cried George,
and then he laughed too.

Other Gullane Children's Books for you to enjoy

Tabitha's Terrifically Tough Tooth
Charlotte Middleton

The Smallest Hero
Gillian Rogerson
illustrated by
Ingela Peterson

Blot and Og's Monster Party
Tasha Pym
illustrated by
Charles Fuge

Big Bad Wolf Is Good
Simon Puttock
illustrated by
Lynne Chapman

Small Florence
Claire Alexander

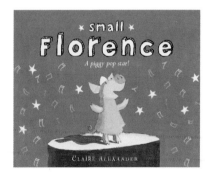